The Sleepover Club

Sleepover Girls on Horseback

by Fiona Cummings

Collins

An imprint of HarperCollinsPublishers

The Sleepover Club ® is a Registered Trademark
of HarperCollins*Publishers* Ltd

First published in Great Britain by Collins in 1998
Collins is an imprint of HarperCollins*Publishers* Ltd
77-85 Fulham Palace Road, Hammersmith,
London, W6 8JB

1 3 5 7 9 8 6 4 2

Text copyright © Fiona Cummings 1998

Original series characters, plotting
and settings © Rose Impey 1997

ISBN 0 00 675391 4

The author asserts the moral right to
be identified as the author of the work.

Printed and bound in Great Britain by
Caledonian International Book Manufacturing Ltd,
Glasgow G64

Sleepover Kit List

1. Sleeping bag
2. Pillow
3. Pyjamas or a nightdress
4. Slippers
5. Toothbrush, toothpaste, soap etc
6. Towel
7. Teddy
8. A creepy story
9. Food for a midnight feast: something
   that horses like to eat, to fit in
   with the horsey theme
10. Torch
11. Hairbrush
12. Hair things like a bobble or hairband,
    if you need them
13. Clean knickers and socks
14. Sleepover diary

PLUS: Stuff to sell at The Sale!!!

CHAPTER ONE

Hi there. Do you want to come and see the horses with me? That's where I'm going now. Look, I know you're thinking, Lyndz is going to bore us with all that dreary stable stuff! The rest of the Sleepover Club used to think that as well. *And* tut and sigh and make neighing noises. But not any more. Not after our latest adventure. In fact, they're coming to see the horses too. I'm going to meet them there – honest!

I haven't told you before, but I have a riding lesson once a week and I help out at the local stables whenever I can. I don't talk about it *too* much in front of the others because they start getting bored and yawn a lot. Still, when you hear about their riding experiences, it's not surprising really. Take Fliss for a start.

Whenever I even *mention* mucking out, she puts her hands over her ears and starts squealing. She's far too anxious about staying clean and tidy to get involved in things like that! Actually I enjoy all those bits – the mucking out and the grooming – almost as much as the riding. You feel kind of close to the horses and they smell all sort of sweet and leathery and warm.

Sorry, there I go again! Where was I? Oh yes, Fliss. She can be a bit of a wimp sometimes and she actually admits that she's frightened of horses. I suppose I *can* sort of understand that – they are kind of big. But they're just so gentle! Even Fliss understands that now, but boy did she find out the hard way! I think we all feel a bit guilty about what happened, but she's OK now.

Frankie is more sensible. She went for riding lessons with Kenny once. Can you imagine that? Kenny on a horse acting the fool and pretending to be a cowboy! It was all "Yee-ha!" and "Hi Ho, Silver!"

You know Kenny: she always wants to do everything as fast as she can. She expected to be out hacking on her first lesson and jumping fences by her second. She just didn't realise that riding isn't like that. It's all about communicating with the horse. You and the horse have to work as a team. Riding is *very* hard work. And Kenny doesn't like hard work at the best of times. So she gave up.

Frankie lasted a bit longer, but you could tell that she wasn't in love with horses in the way I am. I think you really *do* have to love them to want to work at getting everything right. You have so much to think about – squeezing your legs here, holding the reins there, sitting just so. It's not just about trotting along and looking pretty. Which is just as well because I *never* look pretty.

That's what my four stupid brothers tell me anyway. Even Spike, and he's only a baby!

Rosie is the fifth member of the Sleepover Club and she didn't take to riding either. She went along after her brother, Adam, started. You rememer Adam, don't you? He's a year older than Rosie and has cerebral palsy. Riding is a form of therapy for him. He started going once a week with his school and when his mum realised how much it was helping him, she arranged for him to go with two of his friends on another afternoon.

He rides at the same stables as me. Mrs McAllister, who owns it, is a qualified instructor for the Riding for the Disabled Association. She's brilliant because as well as knowing everything there is to know about horses, she knows exactly what kind of horse someone like Adam needs to ride. She says that a little pony like Bramble would have too choppy a stride, so he goes on Marvel, who is a chestnut mare. Her walk is much smoother, but Adam still has to squeeze his legs very hard to make her obey his commands. And when you think about it that's really tough for Adam because he spends all day in a wheelchair so he's not using his leg muscles at all. Just balancing on Marvel gives him a really tough workout.

Crikey, I sound like some kind of doctor, don't I? Kenny would be proud of me!

Adam was so thrilled about riding Marvel, he told Rosie all about it. Of course, *she* wanted to have a go then. She was put on Alfie, the most gorgeous bay with a white star on his forehead and eyelashes to die for, but poor Rosie just couldn't get it together at all. First she had trouble mounting him, then her legs wouldn't stay in the right position in the stirrups. And Alfie just did his own thing, no matter what Rosie tried to tell him to do. In the end she told her mum that riding wasn't for her and she never went again.

I bet you're wondering what this has to do with our latest adventure, aren't you? Well, quite a lot actually – come with me to the stables and I'll tell you all about it on the way.

It started when we were round at Rosie's one afternoon after school. We were working on some dumb geography project.

"I don't know why Mrs Weaver doesn't just send us all on holiday if she wants us to find out about other countries," snarled Kenny, stuffing yet another chocolate biscuit into her mouth.

"Yes, I wouldn't mind a week on the beach in Barbados," sighed Frankie.

"Or a trip to Disneyland!" yelled Fliss.

"That's not a country, stupid!" laughed Kenny.

"I know that, smartypants!" snapped Fliss. "I've been to EuroDisney. I'd just like to go to Disneyland in America to see if it's any different, that's all!"

"Ooh! Hark at her!" we all screeched together, pulling faces at each other.

Fliss hates it when we make fun of her, even though she usually deserves it. She flung her pencil case at Kenny and all her felt pens sort of burst out, scattering around the kitchen. We all creased up and scrambled on to the floor to pick them up. We were scrabbling about under the table, when we heard the front door close.

"That'll be Mum and Adam," said Rosie.

We waited for Adam to burst into the kitchen in his wheelchair like he usually did. But he didn't. All we could hear were lots of strange wailing sounds coming from the hall.

"Oh no!" gasped Rosie. "That's Adam. It sounds like he's really upset about something."

We rushed into the hall to see what was wrong. Rosie's mum was crouched over Adam, trying to calm him down, but we could tell just by looking at him that something awful had happened.

"What is it, Mum? What's wrong?" asked Rosie anxiously. "Is Adam OK?"

Her mum nodded, but carried on stroking Adam's arm. "He's just heard some bad news," she said softly.

"What sort of bad news?" shrieked Rosie. She'd gone completely white and her eyes looked as though they were going to burst out of her head. The rest of us sort of hung back in case it was a private thing.

"We've just heard that there's been a very bad fire at the riding school," said Rosie's mum.

"Oh no!" I gasped. For a minute I felt as though I couldn't breathe. I sat down on the stairs. "What happened? Are the horses safe?" I asked. My voice sounded kind of wobbly. It didn't sound like my voice at all.

"Yes, Lyndz, the horses were in the fields when it happened. And they're all perfectly safe."

"What about Mrs McAllister, is she all right?" asked Frankie.

"Yes, everyone is fine, thank goodness," sighed Mrs Cartwright. "It could have been much worse. Just imagine what would have happened if the horses had been in the stables when the fire started."

I didn't want to imagine that. All I could

think of was Marvel and Alfie and Bramble and all the other beautiful horses. What was going to happen to them now? It felt like the worst day of my life.

When Rosie's mum had taken Adam upstairs for his bath, we went back into the kitchen. It was as though a huge grey blanket of sadness had been dropped on top of us. Nobody spoke for ages.

"There must be *something* we can do to help," I said suddenly. I couldn't bear the silence any longer and just thinking that we could be useful in some way made me feel a bit better. "Let's go to the stables and see what we can do."

"Shouldn't we call Mrs McAllister first?" asked Fliss. "Maybe she won't want anyone there."

"Fliss is right," agreed Frankie. "Why don't you ring Mrs McAllister when you get home, Lyndz, and if she wants us to help, we'll all come to the stables with you later in the week, won't we?"

Everyone nodded. Everyone except Fliss.

"You'll come and help too, won't you, Fliss?" Frankie dug her hard in the ribs.

"Ouch! I suppose so. But I don't want to go anywhere near the horses," said Fliss, rubbing her side.

"OK, that's agreed. You check things with Mrs McAllister, Lyndz. Then it's the Sleepover Club to the rescue!" laughed Kenny and pretended to play a fanfare.

We all laughed too. It sounded like one of our silly jokes. Only this time it was real.

CHAPTER TWO

"Well, what did she say?" The others crowded round me when I got to school the next day.

"Who?" I pretended to look blank, but I couldn't fool them.

"Mrs McAllister of course! Come on, Lyndz. Spill!" commanded Frankie.

"Mum rang her for me," I admitted. "She thought that Mrs McAllister might be in a state of shock."

Kenny's eyes lit up at the thought of some medical-type complaint to deal with.

"And was she?" she asked eagerly.

"Nope, it sounded like she was very calm actually," I said.

Kenny looked disappointed.

"When did the fire start?" asked Frankie, getting down to serious matters.

"Quite early in the morning. The horses were in the fields and Mrs McAllister had gone to check on them," I explained. "She said that something caught her eye. She looked up and saw smoke coming from the stable block. She ran back to see what was happening, but when she got there, three of the stables had burnt completely and the roofs on the others were still burning. She called the fire brigade, grabbed the fire extinguishers, and put out what she could."

"But what caused the fire to start in the first place?" asked Fliss.

"Mrs McAllister doesn't know for sure. She thinks a delivery man must have dropped a cigarette," I told them. "There are huge 'No Smoking' signs all around the stables – how could anyone be so careless?" I looked round and realised that for once I had everyone's attention. And knowing the Sleepover Club you realise what a miracle that is. We usually all chatter at once.

"Do you think someone did it on purpose?" asked Kenny suddenly. "Someone might want to get rid of the riding school! Maybe the owner of a rival stables is trying to close down all the competition so everyone will have to go to them for riding lessons."

Uh-oh! Kenny was on one of her fantasy trips again.

"Get real!" laughed Frankie. "I don't know if you've noticed, but we live in Cuddington, not Hollywood. Things like that don't happen around here."

The others started to laugh and tease Kenny.

"Hey, Lyndz, are you all right?" asked Rosie. "You've gone very quiet."

I'd tried to be bright and happy and everything. But I kept thinking of something else that mum had said last night. She'd asked Mrs McAllister where the horses were being kept.

"On Mr Brocklehurst's farm – for the moment," she'd told her.

That was great news for me, because my brother, Stuart, helps out there. And the horses have always grazed in some of Mr Brocklehurst's fields anyway.

"Aw, we could have had some of the horses to stay here in our garden!" I'd said. Wouldn't that have been great? We've got a huge garden and I'd have looked after them ever so well.

"They might have to live in someone's garden if what Mrs McAllister says is true," Mum had told me. "She says that rebuilding the stables is going to cost thousands of pounds – she just doesn't have that kind of money and only some of it is covered by insurance. She needs the horses settled before winter, so it looks like she might have to close down the riding school and sell the horses."

I had been so upset that I'd hardly slept. And I nearly started crying when I told the others.

"But what about Adam?" Rosie blurted out. "He was upset enough about the fire. I don't know how he'll cope if he can't ride any more."

"Mrs McAllister's going to carry on with her lessons for the moment," I told her. "The practice ring wasn't damaged and it's right next to the farm so the horses can get there easily."

"Are there any other stables nearby?" Fliss asked.

"None that do Riding for the Disabled," Rosie said. "Mum's already asked."

"I don't want to go to another stables. I want to go to that one!" I shouted. The others looked shocked. They're not used to seeing me get upset. But then, nothing has ever threatened the horses before.

"OK, OK, calm down." Frankie took control, as usual. "I'm sure there's *something* we can do."

But before we could come up with a plan, the bell went for the start of school.

"Right you lot, this is Operation Horseback!" shouted Frankie in her Sergeant-Major voice. "*Rendez-vous* here at 10.30 hours (that means first break, dummies). And get your brains into gear for a plan of action. Right you 'orrible lot. Quick march – left, right, left, right…" and we all marched into the classroom.

We would have marched right to our chairs, but Mrs Weaver gave us one of her looks. Sometimes she has no sense of humour. I think she must have had one of her headaches.

I tried to concentrate on my work but I couldn't. I just had to think of a way to save Mrs McAllister's riding school. Every time I looked across at Rosie she seemed to be deep in thought, too. Fliss was staring into space a lot, but I think that was just because she couldn't understand the maths we were doing.

At first break we all met up in the playground.

"Any ideas?" asked Frankie.

We all shook our heads.

"If we were on one of those dumb TV programmes, we'd rebuild the stables ourselves!" she sighed. "But I can't see us being much good at that."

"It's a pity they don't have a Stable Building badge in Brownies. We could have done it for that!" laughed Kenny. She jumped on Frankie's back and pretended to ride her round the playground.

"No horseplay, girls! Someone will get hurt!" shouted out Mrs Daniels.

Frankie had a fit of the giggles. "Horseplay!" she screamed. "Horseplay!"

She was laughing so much that Kenny couldn't hold on and fell to the ground. But she was laughing too, so it didn't matter.

"I bet Danny-Boy didn't even say it on purpose," Kenny snorted. "She's had a sense of humour bypass that woman!"

"We don't have to actually *build* the stables, do we?" said Fliss, suddenly concerned.

"What?" asked the rest of us together.

"Talk about a sense of humour bypass, Fliss – were you operated on too?" asked Kenny.

"No, stupid!" said Fliss going pink. "What I meant was, it's not *building* the stables that's the problem, is it? You said that Mrs McAllister doesn't have any money. So really we should try to find her someone who has."

"Right, Fliss. I'll just write to the Queen shall I?" said Kenny. "*Dear Queenie, the stables where our friends ride have been burnt down. Please send us lots of money so that we can build some more. Lots of love, the Sleepover Club.* That should do the trick, shouldn't it? Ten pound notes will be falling through the letter box in no time!"

"Ha, ha, ha!" said Fliss, going pinker than ever. "That's not what I meant, but there must be *someone* who can help."

"Fliss is right," said Frankie. "Why don't we think of ways to raise money?"

"But we'd never raise enough!" said Fliss.

"That's not the point," said Frankie firmly.

"Every little helps. I'm sure there are lots of people who don't know that the stables have burnt down. If we can 'raise people's awareness', as Mum says, maybe they'll make a donation and Mrs McAllister will get enough money to rebuild her stables."

Suddenly I felt cheerful again. It really seemed as though we *could* make a difference. And more importantly, it looked as though Alfie, Bramble and Marvel wouldn't have to be sold to someone else.

"I'm going to the farm after school tomorrow," I told the others. "I'll tell Mrs McAllister that we're going to help. I'm sure she'll be pleased."

"We'll all come with you, Lyndz," said Frankie. "If the Sleepover Club are going to the rescue, we really should find out what we're rescuing!"

"Yeah!" shouted Kenny and Rosie, doing high fives.

"Are you coming too?" I asked Fliss. She was being very quiet and I knew she wasn't wild about horses. "You don't have to if you don't want to."

"Of course I am!" she said crossly. "You're not leaving me out!"

So we arranged to meet at Mr Brocklehurst's farm after school the next day. It seemed like such a good idea at the time. We should have realised then that Fliss and horses really don't mix!

CHAPTER THREE

I was really excited about going to Mr Brocklehurst's farm the next day, but I was kind of nervous too. I hadn't seen the horses since the fire you see. What if they'd changed? What if they were really spooked by what had happened and wouldn't let anyone near them?

"Are you sure the horses are all right?" I asked Stuart, as Dad drove us to the farm.

"For the hundredth time, Lyndz, they're fine," Stuart replied.

That made me feel a bit better, but butterflies were still flapping about inside my tummy. I know it sounds crazy, but it's just because I love those horses more than anything else in the world and I was worried that they'd be feeling frightened because their routine had changed. Horses are creatures of habit you see.

When we arrived at the farm, I said bye to Dad and jumped out to open the gate. The first thing I saw was Alfie in the field. He was munching grass as usual and didn't look worried at all.

"Happy now?" asked Stuart.

"Yep!" I nodded.

"Oh look, isn't that one of your mad friends?" Stuart pointed to the lane leading to the practice ring. Rosie was standing there, waving at me like a crazy woman. I started walking towards her. Suddenly, *thud*! Kenny leapt on to my back.

"Hiya, Lyndz! Have I missed anything? I would've got here earlier, but my stupid sister wanted to come too. I had to bribe her to stay away. She took all my chocolate and made me promise to help with the washing up for a week!" Kenny was all out of breath and red in the face. And so was I, with such a great lump on top of me!

"Gerroff!" I yelled and threw her off.

"Girls! That's not very lady-like behaviour!" said a loud voice behind us. It sounded just like Mrs Poole, our headmistress. I turned round in a panic, but it was only Frankie. She's dead good at voices.

"What are you doing? I thought we were supposed to be asking Mrs McAllister how we could help," said Frankie. She can be too serious sometimes. She'd probably chill out a bit more if she had brothers and sisters to deal with. I'm always telling her that she can have *my* brothers any time!

"I don't think she'd like us disturbing her now. She's taking a ride with Adam and his friends," said Rosie.

We had walked back down the path and were standing by the field, looking at Alfie.

"All that stuff in the ring is so boring!" said Kenny. "You see Alfie? I bet I could make him jump over that fence – no problem!"

"Oh yeah!" Frankie and Rosie said, laughing.

I don't trust Kenny sometimes. She has a wild streak in her and you just don't know what she's going to do next. I could tell that she was in Grand National mode and I had to get her away from Alfie – fast! Fortunately, just then Stuart walked past, wearing his big wellies and smelling of pigs.

"You're not frightening the horses are you?" he shouted.

"Ha, ha, ha!" we said together.

"Actually," he said, coming over to us, "what exactly *are* you doing here? You're not planning anything are you, Lyndz? I have to work here, remember. I don't want you causing any trouble."

"As if!" I said. He snorted and walked off.

We climbed on to the fence and sat looking at Alfie as he munched away at the grass.

"Did you know that horses graze between sixteen and twenty hours a day?" I asked.

"That sounds nice. I could manage that myself!" laughed Kenny.

"It's because they've got small stomachs you see. They can't cope with big meals," I explained.

"Sounds like Fliss, she's always nibbling at her food!" laughed Rosie. "She hasn't got such big teeth though. And I've never seen her eat grass."

"I bet her mum has!" said Frankie. "She's always going on those weird diets, and there can't be many calories in grass!"

"Speaking of Fliss, where is she?" I asked. "Do you think she's chickened out of coming after all?"

"Horsied out you mean!" shrieked Kenny.

I don't know why, but that really made me laugh. And you know what happens when I laugh too much, don't you? Yep, I got the dreaded hiccups.

"Aw, Lyndz, look, you're frightening Alfie!" laughed Rosie.

Alfie was looking at me through his long eyelashes. He didn't look very impressed.

31

But that only made me laugh more. Frankie grabbed hold of my hand to give me her evil 'thumb in the hand' routine. I was trying to balance on the fence, holding on with only one arm. It wasn't very easy. What I didn't need was someone running up behind me and digging me in the ribs. Which is exactly what Fliss did.

"Lyndz, I'm here!" she shouted.

Thump! I fell off the fence. *Splat*! Right on top of Fliss.

She lay on the ground covered in bits of hay. And pig muck, by the smell of her.

"Lyndz, you clumsy thing! Look at me!" she wailed. "I wasn't going to come in the first place. I wish I hadn't bothered now!"

"I'm sorry, Fliss. I couldn't help it!" I said, pulling her to her feet. "But at least it got rid of my hiccups!"

"Well, that's all right then!" grumbled Fliss.

The rest of us looked at Fliss and started to laugh. She was covered in muddy marks and nasty brown splodges. It wouldn't have been so bad if she'd been wearing scruffy old jeans and wellies like the rest of us. But that's not Fliss's style. Instead, she had on her black Adidas top, new pink bootleg trousers and some high-heeled boots.

"Fliss what *are* you like!" laughed Kenny. "This isn't a photo shoot for *Vogue* you know. You're supposed to be mucking in!"

"Fliss has been mucking in!" shrieked Rosie. "*Pig* mucking in!"

We screamed with laughter again. But we soon stopped when it looked as though Fliss was going to cry.

"I didn't have any old jeans, Mum's given them all away," she spluttered. "And I need some new wellies as well. My feet are too big for the ones I've got."

"You should have said," said Rosie. "I've got some old ones that will probably fit you. *And* some old jeans. They're in a pile waiting for Mum to take to the charity shop."

"I wish I'd known," said Fliss, trying to brush the marks from her trousers. "Anyway, have you come up with a plan to

33

raise millions of pounds yet?"

"Nope!" said Kenny, Rosie and I.

"Yes!" shouted Frankie. "Yes, yes, yes!"

We all stared at her with our mouths open.

"I am Brain of Britain. I should have a medal!" she laughed, dancing about. "Don't you see? It's brilliant. We've all got things that we don't need any more, but which someone else probably does. Instead of taking them to the charity shop, *we* can sell them. And the money we make can go towards the Save the Stables campaign. Genius, or what?"

"But how will people find out that we have things to sell?" asked Fliss.

"We'll make posters and put them up all over Cuddington," replied Frankie.

"We need to do it as soon as possible," I said. "The sooner we raise money the better."

Frankie started jumping up and down. She was going quite pink with excitement. "We're having a sleepover at my place next

Friday, aren't we? How about having a sale the next day? In our garden."

"Yes!" we all said together.

"Won't your mum mind?" asked Fliss, nervously.

"Nah! It's for a good cause, and Mum believes in good causes," Frankie replied. "She might even donate some stuff herself."

"Look!" I said. "Mrs McAllister is just coming back from the lesson with Adam. Let's tell her what we're going to do."

Mrs McAllister was leading Adam on Marvel. He looked very tired, but happy. We told her about our plan, all talking at the same time and shouting to make ourselves heard. She just sort of smiled sadly, but Adam became quite excited.

"What's he saying?" we asked Rosie's mum, who had just turned up.

She interpreted the gestures Adam made with his head and arms. "He says that he'll do the posters on his computer for you!" she announced.

"Coo-el!" we all cried. Adam's brilliant at

stuff like that.

"Well, I'm not sure how much good it will do," said Mrs McAllister sadly, "but it's great that you're taking such an interest. I hope it goes well."

"Is there anything you'd like us to do now?" I asked.

"Well, these horses need feeding. Then of course there's the mucking out!" she said.

"Sorry, my dad's here," said Frankie, hurrying away. "You're coming with me, aren't you, Kenny?" Kenny laughed and ran off as well, waving at me as she went.

"We've got to get back too, haven't we, Mum?" said Rosie, pushing Adam towards the car.

"That leaves you and me, Fliss!" I laughed.

"Sorry, Lyndz, Mum's coming for me in five minutes. I think I'll just go and wait by the gate," squealed Fliss, moving away.

Unfortunately, while we had been talking, I hadn't noticed that Marvel had taken a fancy to Fliss's Adidas top. As she walked away there was a loud rip, and a great chunk of black material came away in Marvel's mouth.

You should have seen the look on her face! That should really have been a sign that Fliss should be kept away from horses for good. But unfortunately for Fliss, we didn't take any notice.

CHAPTER FOUR

I was quite tired when I arrived home from the farm. Mucking out horses is hard work you know. For once I didn't have any homework to do, only reading, and I always do that in bed. I just planned to have something to eat and then flop in front of the TV. Bliss!

"There you are, boss!" said Mum as soon as I walked through the door. "I was wondering when you were going to get back. I hope you're going to pay me for being your secretary!"

She's really lost it this time, I thought to

myself. I mean, I know that Mum has a hard time working and looking after five children, but what *was* she on about?

"Your friends have been phoning for the last hour! I thought you were going to see them at the farm," she said.

"I did," I replied, puzzled.

"I wrote down their messages and put them on your desk—"

I started to run up to my bedroom.

"Not so fast, young lady," she called. "Wash your hands and come for supper first. The rest of us are starving!"

I gobbled down my supper so quickly it was a record, even for me. When I rushed into my bedroom, my desk was covered in post-it notes. Mum had stuck them in a line so I knew which order to read them in. The first message read:

From Frankie:
What happened to Fliss's top? I was going to come back to find out, but Kenny wouldn't let me in case we got roped into mucking out!

The next note said:

Can Lyndz come over to my place after school tomorrow? Adam wants to find out what we want him to put on the posters – Rosie

Mum had written underneath:

WHICH POSTERS? WHAT ARE YOU UP TO, LYNDSEY COLLINS?

The next message was from Kenny:

Are you going to Rosie's tomorrow? I am, and Frankie is too. Have you spoken to Fliss since her 'horsey' experience? Ha, ha, ha! (That was Kenny laughing.)
I HOPE YOU'RE NOT UPSETTING FLISS AGAIN. I TOLD KENNY THAT YOU COULD GO TO ROSIE'S AFTER SCHOOL. SHE TOLD ME ABOUT THE POSTERS AND THE SALE TO RAISE MONEY FOR THE STABLES. PERHAPS YOU CAN GET RID OF SOME OF THAT JUNK IN YOUR BEDROOM – MUM

The last message was from Fliss:

Mum nearly killed me when she saw the state of my top. She said she always knew that horses were dangerous and she doesn't want me getting mixed up with them. I don't think she's even going to let me go to Rosie's tomorrow – or Frankie's sleepover next week.

I felt really bad when I read that. It was sort of my fault that Fliss had ended up getting so dirty. And if I'd been watching properly, Marvel would never have eaten her top.

There was a knock at my bedroom door. Mum came in.

"Mum, I don't know what to do—" I began.

She handed me another post-it note. It read:

I'VE SPOKEN TO FLISS'S MUM. FLISS CAN GO TO ROSIE'S AND FRANKIE'S. JUST KEEP HER AWAY FROM HORSES FOR GOODNESS' SAKE! – MUM xxx

I read her note and smiled. I grabbed a pen and wrote on the bottom:

Thanks, Mum. You're the best!

When we saw each other at school the next day, we didn't really talk about what had happened at the farm. All our parents had told us to be nice to Fliss, so we didn't want to upset her again. I think she was a bit embarrassed about it too, because she never mentioned it either. And you know Fliss, she usually goes on and on about stuff.

After school we all walked back to Rosie's house. Tiff, her older sister, looks after her until her mum gets back. Her mum's at college at the moment, you see. She's training to be a nursery assistant. She also has to go and pick up Adam from school, so she always gets home a bit later than Rosie.

When we got to her house, Rosie gave us all some Coca-Cola. We put some crisps into a bowl and took them up to her bedroom. Her room's enormous, but it's still not decorated. That's cool because it means we can write on the walls, but she's nearly run out of wall to write on now.

"What are you going to take to the sale?" Frankie asked Rosie.

"I don't know, clothes I suppose," she replied. "I don't really have anything else that I want to get rid of. What about you?"

"Toys that I don't need any more," Frankie said. "I've kept them in case I got a baby brother or sister to give them to, but I don't suppose I ever will now."

The rest of us looked at each other and pulled faces. Frankie could go on for hours about how unfair it is being an only child.

"What are you going to sell, Lyndz?" Kenny asked me, trying to change the subject.

"Dunno," I shrugged. "Mum reckons that I should sell some of the junk I've got in my bedroom. She just doesn't realise that I need it all."

"Same with me," admitted Kenny. "My mum doesn't see why I have to keep all my old football magazines and programmes and stuff. I keep telling her that one day I'll be able to sell them and make a fortune."

"Yeah, right!" I laughed. "Like who would want them?"

A word of warning to you – NEVER criticise Kenny's obsession with Leicester City Football Club. It's just not worth it!

"All right then," she said, looking very angry. "Why are you holding on to all your old posters and horse magazines? If you cared so much about Mrs McAllister's horses, you'd sell them to raise money for the stables."

Aargh! What she was saying was true, but I didn't want to get rid of them.

"All right, I'll sell them," I told her bravely. "As long as you sell your football stuff."

Kenny went bright red. She realised that she'd talked herself into trouble. But Kenny never likes to admit that she's wrong.

"All right, I will!" she said.

Frankie, Rosie and Fliss looked at each other, but they didn't dare say anything. Kenny and I looked at each other. I felt bad and I knew that Kenny did too, but we couldn't go back on our word now.

Just then, we heard the front door open and the sound of Adam's wheelchair speeding across the hall floor.

"We'd better go down," said Rosie. "Adam will be dying to get on with the posters."

We trooped downstairs, still hardly daring to speak to each other.

"Hi, Adam. Have you had a good day?" asked Frankie.

Adam nodded and smiled his big smile. He wheeled himself over to his computer and we all crowded round.

"Right. What shall we put on these posters?" he gestured.

"We'll have to say what the sale's in aid of," I said.

"As briefly as possible," added Frankie. "We need a catchy slogan or something. Why don't you put 'Save our horses' at the top?"

Adam tapped away on his computer.

"Next write that the sale's at my house, on Saturday," said Frankie. "And the time. What do you think about starting at ten and going on till twelve? Will that give us enough time to get everything ready?"

We all nodded.

"You should call it a car boot sale," said Fliss. "People always go to those."

"But it's not is it? There won't *be* any cars there," laughed Kenny. "It's more like a wellington boot sale!"

"Just put 'Grand sale of almost new items'," said Frankie, "and then 'Please support this worthwhile cause' along the bottom."

"We could print them on coloured paper," Rosie suggested. "We want as many people to see them as possible." She put some fluorescent pink paper into the printer, and hey presto! our first poster emerged. It looked awesome:

SAVE OUR HORSES

Help prevent the closure of
McAllister's Riding School

GRAND SALE
OF ALMOST NEW
ITEMS

at

7 The Ridgeway
Melford Road
Cuddington

Saturday 12th September
10 am - 12 noon
Please support this worthwhile cause

"Adam, you're a genius. Much like myself!" laughed Frankie.

"It's brilliant!" I agreed.

"Coo-el!" the others cheered.

"Now we need to put up as many as possible," said Kenny. "We want to make sure that everyone sees one."

Adam printed off a whole load of posters and we took ten each. We figured that as we all live in different parts of the village, between us we should have the area pretty much covered.

Big mistake!

Why do none of our plans ever turn out the way we want them to?

CHAPTER FIVE

You'd think that it would be easy to get rid of ten posters wouldn't you? Well it wasn't. A lot of the shops in the village actually charge for putting them up in their windows, which is crazy if you ask me.

Frankie decided that she didn't want to put up any posters in school either.

"Why not?" we all asked.

"Because of the M&Ms," she replied. "You know what they're like. They'll spoil it for us."

She was right. The M&Ms – better known as Emma Hughes and Emily Berryman – are our deadly rivals. In front of grown-ups they act so goody-goody it's sickening, but in fact they try to spoil everything we do. We usually get the better of them, but I suppose Frankie was right – we couldn't take the risk this time.

In the end, I put up two posters just outside the school gates. I gave a poster to Ben to put up in his nursery class (but I think he scribbled all over it first), I gave two to Mrs McAllister to put up somewhere at the stables, and stuck the rest on lampposts in our road.

But putting up posters about the sale was the least of my worries. I still had to decide what I was going to sell. I had promised to donate some of my horse posters, but I couldn't decide which ones. I know it sounds silly, but it's as though the horses in the posters are real somehow, so it was really hard for me to decide which ones to give away.

I kept getting out the posters from under my bed and sorting them into two piles –

ones that I loved, and ones that I really really loved. The only problem was that I always ended up with two posters in the first pile, and about thirty-six in the second. Then I felt guilty about leaving those two out to start with, so I put them back with the others anyway. I'm not very good at making decisions.

In the end, Mum helped me make up my mind. She said that the sensible thing to do would be to keep only the most recent posters. The important thing was not to look at them too closely, just decide how long I'd had them.

In the end I had a big pile to take to the sale and a smaller pile to keep. Once I'd decided which posters were going, I put them in a plastic bag and didn't look at them again. Then I did the same thing with all my horse magazines. I felt sad about getting rid of them, but fortunately I had something to take my mind off it. On the Tuesday before her sleepover, Frankie had come rushing into the playground.

"I've had a brilliant idea!" she announced.

"Not another one!" we groaned.

"No, you'll love this!" she said, looking very pleased with herself.

"We're in for a Frankie Thomas special are we?" laughed Kenny. "Go on then. Spill!"

"Well, you know we're having the sale to raise money for the riding school?" she began.

"Are we?" "What sale?" "I didn't know about that!" the rest of us said, pretending to look shocked.

"Ha, ha, ha!" said Frankie. "Well I thought it would be pretty cool if the sleepover had a horsey theme. We could all wear something connected with horses. We can eat cowboy-type food, even our games could be horsey ones. AND whatever you bring for the midnight feast has to fit into the theme too. What do you think?"

"Brilliant!" I laughed, jumping up and down. This sounded like my kind of party.

"Wicked!" said Rosie and Kenny together.

"I don't understand," said Fliss. "You

mean we've got to dress up as a horse?"

"Derr!" said the rest of us, tapping our heads.

"No, Fliss, you can dress as a cowboy or an Indian if you want. Or wear jodhpurs," explained Frankie. "Just use your imagination."

"But I don't think I've got anything like that to wear," moaned Fliss.

"Oh, come on, Fliss," snapped Kenny. "You've got more clothes than the rest of us put together. I'm sure you can find *something*."

We left it so that we wouldn't tell anyone else what we were wearing. It had to be a surprise on Friday night.

I couldn't wait for the sleepover. I love all our sleepovers of course, because we always end up having a wicked time. But it's even more fun if we have to dress up – and I'm really lucky because I've got some ace dressing-up clothes.

I could have worn the jodhpurs that I wear for riding, but they're a bit dirty and smelly. Besides, Mum once made me some of those leather chaps that cowboys wear over their jeans. I love wearing those, and I knew that Kenny would just about die when she saw them.

So on Friday, when I got ready for the sleepover, I put on the chaps and my checked shirt, and Dad lent me one of his bootlace ties. Then I found a beaten-up old leather hat in the dressing-up box. It sort of looked like a cowboy hat. I thought it was pretty cool anyway. The last thing to do was borrow one of Ben's toy guns. I hid it from Mum though, because she doesn't like him having them.

When Dad dropped me off at Frankie's I was so excited I couldn't get out of the car fast enough. I grabbed my sleepover kit and my bag of horse posters and magazines and rushed up to the door. Kenny was already there, looking like the meanest cowboy in the West.

When she heard me, she spun round and said in a fake American accent, "Not so fast pardn'r. This doorway ain't big enough for the both of us!"

We both dropped our bags and grabbed the guns from our holsters. Then we pretended to have this mega shoot-out down Frankie's path. Suddenly the front door opened.

"All right, Butch and Sundance. You'd better come in before the neighbours call the police!" It was Frankie's dad.

Well, Kenny and I just creased up. And it didn't help when Fliss came tiptoeing down the path looking like Little Bo Peep!

"Hic! What are you like, Fliss?" I giggled.

"I'm a cowgirl!" she said angrily. I could tell that she was in a major strop.

"Oh yes, hic! I see now!" I said. She was wearing a flouncy skirt, a white blouse and ankle boots. She didn't look like a cowgirl at all.

"Frankie!" shouted Mr Thomas. "I think Lyndz needs your assistance. She's got hiccups again!"

Frankie came flying downstairs. She

looked pretty cool in a pair of jodhpurs and a riding jacket. Rosie was behind her. She was dressed like an Indian squaw. She said her mum had made her dress out of chamois-leather cloths! It was wicked!

We all looked at each other, shouting "Coo-el!" We didn't mention the fact that Fliss looked as though she'd escaped from the pages of a nursery-rhyme book.

Frankie tried to get rid of my hiccups, but they just wouldn't go away. Eventually her mum appeared.

"I'll give you five pounds if you hiccup again, Lyndz," she said.

The others all stared at me, willing me to make another sound. But do you know, I couldn't!

"Thought that might happen," laughed Frankie's mum, and disappeared again.

We took our things up to Frankie's room, then Kenny asked, "What's the plan then, Buffalo Bill?"

"We're going to do a spot of show jumping, old girl," said Frankie in a put-on snooty voice.

"Jolly good!" we all laughed and traipsed downstairs again, following Frankie out into the garden.

She'd made a sort of obstacle course with planks of wood and things. Frankie pretended to be a horse and Kenny was her rider, then they had to try to get round the course, jumping the fences without falling over. It was hysterical to watch – and even more hysterical to do. We all had a go at being the horse and the rider. Even Fliss, which was a surprise. It was even more surprising when she was quite good at it!

When we'd finished, we flopped on the grass for a bit to get our breath back. Then we played our game where we get into two teams, with one horse and one rider on each team, and each team has to try to knock the other one over. We play that a lot, but this time Frankie said it was like jousting so it was an OK horsey-type game. I was ready for something to eat after that – it's pretty exhausting.

It was getting dark and Frankie's dad had built a small fire in the corner of the garden. We sat round it and helped to cook baked beans and vegebangers. It was wicked!

"We're just like cowboys!" laughed Kenny.

"I expect the plains of America are a bit more rugged than our back garden," said Frankie's dad. "Hang on a minute though." He rushed behind the dustbins and started to howl like a wolf.

"Yes, that's definitely more like it!" said Mrs Thomas, shaking her head and pulling faces at us. "It keeps him happy!" she whispered.

After the baked beans, we toasted marshmallows on long skewers until they were dripping and tasted a bit smoky. Scrummy!

We were all starting to feel a bit drowsy, but Frankie had one more thing for us to do. And this was no game. This was Organising Tomorrow's Big Sale.

CHAPTER SIX

We headed up to Frankie's room and sat on her bed. Frankie took a sheet of paper from her desk. "Look, this is what I thought we'd do tomorrow," she said.

We all crowded round to have a look. It was a sort of timetable:

Get up/breakfast	8 am
Set out tables in garden	9 am
First customers	10 am
Sold up, made lots of money, exhausted and happy!	Midday
Count money	12.10 pm
Clear away	12.20 pm
Chill out, pig out until we're stuffed!	12.40 pm

"Wicked!" we all laughed. "Especially the pigging out bit!"

"So what's everyone going to sell?" asked Frankie.

I raced over to the bunk beds, grabbed the bag containing my posters and magazines and took it back to Frankie's bed. The others were clutching their bags too.

"OK, after three, everyone tip their stuff out!" commanded Kenny. "One... two... three!"

Posters, make-up, toys and clothes spilled out over the bed.

"I hope everything's clean!" said Fliss, picking things up and shaking them as though they were full of dust.

"We don't seem to have much!" said Frankie. She looked very disappointed.

"There are only five of us, Frankie!" said Rosie. "There's only so much stuff we could get rid of."

"Speaking of which," I said, "there don't seem to be many football things here, Kenny."

She gave me an evil stare.

"That's because they're all here," said Frankie. She fished under her bed and found another plastic bag. She tipped lots of posters and programmes on to the bed. There were even a couple of old books about football too.

"Were you trying to hide those, Kenny?" asked Rosie.

"No, I er… well, all right, yes. I just wanted to make sure that Lyndz had brought her horse posters, that's all," Kenny admitted.

We all laughed. Poor Kenny, you just knew it had almost broken her heart to part with so much stuff!

"Well I reckon we'll only need three tables tomorrow," said Frankie, taking charge again. "One for the books and posters, that's you, Kenny and Lyndz. One for the clothes and make-up – that will be yours, Rosie and Fliss. And then I'll just need a small one for my toys."

"That's not fair!" moaned Fliss. "Everyone will notice your things because they'll be on their own."

"All right, you have the small table then," sighed Frankie.

"No, it's OK," said Fliss after a while. "I think I'd rather be with Rosie."

We all tutted. It was typical of Fliss always to want something else, just to be difficult.

With all our arrangements for the next day sorted out, we got ready for bed.

"What if no one comes," said Fliss when we were all in bed.

"Of course people will come!" snapped Kenny. "People always love buying things."

"I hope so, because if we don't raise money soon, the riding school will close for sure," I said.

"We've got to be positive!" said Frankie.

"Well *I'm* positive," said Rosie. "Positive that it's time for our midnight feast!"

We all whooped and grabbed our 'horsey' food supplies. I'd brought Wagon Wheels (you know, cowboys and all that), Fliss had brought apples, Rosie had brought Polo mints and Frankie had sliced up some carrots – all the things that horses like to eat as treats. Kenny had brought an enormous packet of chip-sticks and some Twiglets.

"What have they got to do with horses?" asked Frankie.

"The chip-sticks look a bit like hay and the Twiglets reminded me of horses' legs!" Kenny replied.

That made us all double over. We were shrieking so much, we didn't hear the knock at the door.

"Crikey, it's so noisy, I thought you'd got one of Mrs McAllister's horses in here with you!" laughed Mrs Thomas, poking her head round the door. "It's time you lot were asleep. I don't want to have to turn away crowds of people tomorrow because you're not up in time for your sale. Goodnight. Sleep tight." She closed the door and turned off the light. We waited a bit and then turned on our torches.

"I hope there *will* be a lot of people," I said.

"Bound to be" reassured Frankie. "They'll

be coming to buy all Kenny's football souvenirs. I heard them announcing it on the news."

The last thing I heard before falling asleep was Kenny trying to strangle Frankie.

The next morning was a bit grey and overcast. Not the perfect day for an outdoor sale.

"At least it's not raining," said Rosie, brightly.

We got dressed as quickly as we could and hurried downstairs. There was a lovely smell of toast wafting up from the kitchen.

"Breakfast's ready, girls!" said Mr Thomas. "I've set up the tables outside for you. What a kind man I am!"

"Thanks, Dad," said Frankie, giving him a big kiss.

We wolfed down our toast and hurried outside. The tables were just inside the garden gate. They were covered in pink material. "Wicked!" we all said.

We brought down our things from

Frankie's room and put the bags on one of the tables.

"Right, which table do you and Rosie want, Fliss?" Frankie asked her. If Fliss chose first, she couldn't complain later. She chose the one nearest the gate.

"Right then, Lyndz and Kenny, you put your things here and I'll have this small table," Frankie commanded.

Kenny and I pulled out our posters and magazines. I took out the Blu-Tack I'd brought with me and stuck some of my posters round the front of the table. Kenny did the same with some of hers. Then we arranged the magazines on top. It actually looked very good.

"What should we charge?" I asked Kenny.

"£1 a poster, 50p a magazine," she replied.

"Don't be stupid, you want to sell them don't you?" said Frankie, who had been listening. "10p and 5p sounds about right. Maybe 25p for a book."

"What about my make-up and jewellery?" asked Fliss. "Some of it was quite expensive you know."

"Yes, but you've used it," said Rosie. "I'm just going to see what people are prepared to pay. Any money is better than nothing."

"That's a good idea," said Frankie. "I might do that too."

"Hey, Frankie, it's ten o'clock!" yelled Kenny. "It's time for the grand opening."

Frankie walked solemnly to the gate. "On behalf of the Sleepover Club," she announced, "I declare this sale well and truly open!"

We all cheered and Frankie very grandly swung open the garden gate. She wasn't exactly knocked down by the rush to get in. In fact only my mum and Spike were there!

"Well, doesn't this look lovely!" Mum said.

"Do you fancy a coffee, Patsy?" Frankie's mum asked and whisked her off into the kitchen.

"Charming!" I said. "I thought she might at least have bought something first."

Spike stayed outside with us, which would have been a disaster if it hadn't been for Frankie's toy elephant. He pulled it from her table and started sucking its ears. Then he started to dig up the garden with its trunk.

"How much do you want for it?" I asked Frankie.

"£1.50?"

I looked in my purse. "I'll give you £1," I said.

"OK. Done!"

£1 was a small price to pay to keep my brother amused.

We could hear people chattering on the footpath. "Quick, more customers!" whispered Frankie.

We all rushed behind our tables and waited eagerly. But it was only Fliss's mum and her step-dad, Andy.

"There aren't many people here are there, darling?" Fliss's mum said to her. Like we really needed to hear that. Then she said, "Maybe you should have put up those posters after all."

We all looked at Fliss.

"How about a cup of coffee, Nikky?" Frankie's mum called from the kitchen.

When her mum and Andy had gone inside, we all turned on Fliss.

"What did your mum mean?" I asked.

Fliss blushed and started stuttering, "Well, I – I did put a poster on our gate and one on the tree next door. B-but Mr Watson-Wade said it made the street look untidy, so I took them down."

"So you didn't put up *any* then?" asked Kenny.

"Well, no, but I haven't seen any of yours either, so I didn't think it mattered."

"NOT MATTERED?" yelled Frankie. "Of course it mattered. How could people find out about the sale if there weren't any posters for them to read?"

"Well, where did *you* put yours then?" Fliss asked Frankie.

"On the gate, on the tree outside, on some lampposts and on a couple of bus shelters," she snapped. "I put up one in my bedroom too. But I didn't expect anyone to see *that* one."

"But we didn't see any of the others either," said Rosie quietly. "And there's definitely not one on the gate now."

Frankie went to look. "I don't believe it, they've gone!" she cried.

No one could remember seeing *any* of our posters at all. But who would have wanted to take them down? And it was obvious that someone had, because nobody was coming to even look at our things.

Our parents turned up of course, but they don't count. And as soon as she saw them, Frankie's mum took them into the kitchen anyway. Adam came and he stayed with us. But he looked so sad when no one turned up, it made us feel even worse.

In the end we bought things from each other, just to make ourselves feel better. I bought another of Frankie's toys, Fliss bought some of Rosie's old jeans (just for going to the farm in), Rosie bought some of Fliss's silver nail varnish and Frankie paid £1 for a whole pile of Kenny's football posters and programmes.

"What do *you* want those for?" Kenny asked her. "I didn't think you liked football."

"I don't," replied Frankie. "I just need some paper to make a papier mâché model with!"

"Oh no you don't!" yelled Kenny, chasing her round the garden.

We all cheered each time they ran past us. Eventually they collapsed, exhausted.

"I'll tell you what, Kenny," gasped Frankie. "You can have your stupid posters back for £1.50."

"No way!"

"Yes way – or the posters get turned to mush!"

Kenny thought about it for about ten seconds. "OK," she grumbled and handed over the money.

Just as we heard the village clock striking twelve, two figures appeared at the gate. It was the M&Ms.

"Oh dear, we haven't missed some kind of sale, have we?" asked Emma Hughes innocently.

"You really should have put up some posters to let people know you were having one," laughed Emily Berryman.

"I just hope no one is relying on you to raise money," said Queen Emma. "We'd hate to think of you letting anyone down!"

And with that the Gruesome Twosome ran cackling down the road.

"*They* must have taken our posters down!" yelled Kenny. "They're going to pay for this!"

CHAPTER SEVEN

You know what Kenny's like. She wanted to run after the M&Ms and sort them out right there and then. But the rest of us had more important things on our mind – like saving the riding school. We all felt we'd let Mrs McAllister down.

We began to pack everything away.

"What are we going to do now?" asked Frankie.

"What *can* we do?" asked Rosie glumly.

"If it hadn't been for those stupid M&Ms tearing down our posters, we'd probably have sold everything and have loads of dosh for the stables by now," shouted Kenny. She was red in the face and she looked MAD.

The sound of raised voices had brought our parents out of the kitchen. I still felt miffed they hadn't bought anything. I know we normally don't like the oldies interfering in our schemes, but this was different. They knew that the whole point of the sale was to raise money.

"That's right! Come out now when we've packed everything away!" Frankie snapped at her mum. It wasn't like her to have a go at her parents. I knew that she must be feeling as bad as me.

"Look, Frankie, I'm sorry that your sale hasn't gone well. We all are," said Mrs Thomas calmly. "But we didn't think that buying your junk was the best way for us to support you. You can have this though." She handed Frankie a tin containing loads of 50p pieces and some £1 coins.

"What's this?" asked Frankie.

"I charged everyone for coffee and

biscuits," laughed her mum. "I'm not stupid!"

"Thanks, Mum," said Frankie. "It's a start, but we need some SERIOUS money now. Any ideas?"

Everyone shook their heads. We were all idea-d out after the disappointment of the sale. Adam was getting very agitated.

"He says that you've got to think of a way to save the horses," interpreted his mother. "Look, why don't you all sleep on it and meet again at our house tomorrow afternoon. Maybe one of you will have come up with a plan by then."

"Fliss won't be home late, will she?" asked her mum anxiously. "I like her to be in bed early on a Sunday night."

Fliss blushed a shade of beetroot, but at least it made the rest of us laugh.

"Is four till six OK?" asked Rosie's mum.

Everyone agreed that it was.

As we collected all our stuff together, it felt like the end of any other sleepover. It was only when Mum was driving me and Spike home that I began to feel really miserable.

What had seemed like such a great plan had gone utterly and horribly wrong.

As soon as I got home I ran up to my room and decided that I wouldn't go down again until I'd thought of a way to save the stables. The trouble was that when I got up there, it seemed an age since breakfast – we hadn't really felt like pigging out when the sale finished after all. My stomach started to rumble and I couldn't think straight because I was so hungry. My brain was as empty as my tummy.

There was a knock at my door. It was Mum to tell me that lunch was ready. When I told her that I was going to stay there until I'd thought of a plan, she came in and sat down on my bed.

"That's an awful lot of responsibility you're putting on those shoulders, Lyndsey," she said to me. "You can't do this by yourself."

"I know, Mum," I told her. "But I've got to try."

"Well what about doing something that

involves the horses?" she suggested. "If people could see how much pleasure they give, maybe they would dig deeper in their pockets. If I were you I'd go and visit Mrs McAllister tomorrow morning and see if you can think of something together."

Mum's a genius sometimes. I gave her a hug and went down for my lunch.

When I arrived at Mr Brocklehurst's farm the next day, I was really excited because I'd been thinking about what Mum had said and I'd had an idea. But I was kind of nervous too because I didn't want to have to tell Mrs McAllister what a disaster the sale had been. I needn't have worried about it though, because when I arrived Adam and Rosie were already there with their mum.

"Hi, Lyndz!" said Rosie when she saw me. "Adam was really miserable so we came to see the horses. We've told Mrs McAllister about the sale and everything and she's been pretty cool about it. Why are *you* here?"

"I've had this idea about organising a big

Stable Fun Day with everybody getting involved with the horses. You know, with gymkhana games and things to do for children," I squealed. The more I thought about it, the better the idea became.

"Cool!" laughed Rosie.

We both danced and hugged each other. And when I told her about it, Mrs McAllister also thought it was a great idea.

We wandered across to the field to look at Bramble for a bit and then went back to the stable block where Mrs McAllister was grooming Alfie. Adam was there too and we all chatted about ideas for the Fun Day.

"I think Adam and his friends should show everybody what they can do," said Mrs McAllister, as she picked out Alfie's hoofs. "A lot of people don't know what Riding for the Disabled is all about. Would you like to show them, Adam?"

Adam nodded and smiled and pointed to Marvel.

"Yes, you can ride Marvel!" laughed Mrs McAllister.

"What can Lyndz do?" asked Rosie.

"Oh, I'm sure there's lots of events she can enter, don't worry!" laughed Mrs McAllister, smiling at me.

"What about my friends?" I asked. "They've got to be involved too!"

"There'll be lots for everyone to do, Lyndsey," Mrs McAllister reassured me. "The main thing is to prove that the riding school is worth saving."

It was lovely being there, thinking that we were actually going to do something to help. I felt really happy and Adam got really excited. He had some brilliant ideas too, like writing to the local newspaper asking them to come and report on the Fun Day.

When it was time to leave, Rosie's mum gave me a lift back home.

"Won't it be cool if we get this planned without the others knowing?" laughed Rosie as I got out of the car. "I can't wait to see their faces when we tell them about it."

And it *was* cool. That afternoon I arrived at Rosie's house early and helped Adam design the new posters. He'd already written the letter he was going to send to *The Leicester Mercury*. You could tell he was really fired up about the idea.

When the others turned up they all had faces like a wet weekend. You just knew that they hadn't had any more money-making ideas. It was really difficult for me and Rosie to keep straight faces. We wanted to burst out and tell them about the Fun Day straight away. But we'd agreed that we should make them sweat a bit first. Cruel or what!

"It's no good!" moaned Fliss. "We've tried our best. Maybe we're just too young for all this."

"Don't be so wet, Fliss," yelled Kenny. "Our ideas are as good as anyone else's."

"It's just that we don't have any," said Frankie sadly.

Rosie and I couldn't stand it any more. Rosie nudged Adam, who was doubled up with laughter himself.

"I don't see what's so funny!" snapped Fliss.

Adam handed them a copy of the new poster:

Help prevent the closure of
McAllister's Riding School

STABLE FUN DAY
Come and have fun with
the horses
Fun for all the family
Events for all abilities
at
Brocklehurst's Farm
Crofter's Lane
Little Wearing
Near Cuddington

Sunday 27th September
10 am – 2 pm

Admission: £3 per adult, £1.50 per child

It was wicked watching their faces as they read the poster.

"This is brilliant!" gasped Frankie. "Who thought of it?"

"Lyndz," beamed Rosie.

I blushed when she said that. I couldn't believe that the Fun Day had been my idea.

"Where are we going to put the posters so the Gruesome Twosome can't sabotage this idea as well?" asked Kenny.

"The M&Ms needn't know we're involved," I said. "Frankie's address was on the other poster, which sort of gave the game away. If the M&Ms ask, we'll just pretend we don't know anything about it. AND we'll keep an eye on the posters we do put up."

"How exactly are we going to be involved?" asked Fliss. "I won't have to ride anything will I?"

"Nobody has to get on a horse if they don't want to," Rosie reassured her. "There'll be lots of ways for us to help. We thought we could take photographs of children sitting on the horses and charge for them."

"But we're hopeless with cameras!" said Frankie.

"Yes, I know!" admitted Rosie. "Mum said she'd take the photographs if we wanted, but I don't know whether we should let the oldies get involved. You know how they take over."

We all nodded.

"I suppose if people are paying money though, they'll want a decent photo and not one of our pathetic efforts," reasoned Frankie. "Besides, we weren't very successful with the sale we organised by ourselves were we?"

We all had to admit that this was true.

"Well, maybe we could let them get involved, just a little," Rosie said. "And one of us could collect the money for the photographs, so we'd still have some control over things."

We spent the rest of the afternoon planning all the things we could do at the Fun Day. Apart from Fliss, who spent most of *her* time planning what she was going to wear!

We took some posters away with us. But

this time we told each other exactly where we were going to put them up. That way we could keep an eye on them.

We were all pretty excited about the Stable Fun Day because it felt as though we were involved in something really big and important. Even Fliss was excited, but I think that was because Adam had told her that a photographer from *The Leicester Mercury* might be there. I think she thought she might be spotted and given a modelling contract or something. Well she certainly got to be on the front page, but not in quite the way she had in mind!

CHAPTER EIGHT

The next two weeks were just one mega-blur of activity. It's a wonder we found time to go to school! We put up posters all around Cuddington. AND checked them every day to make sure they were still there. The M&Ms caught us checking one, but we pretended that we were only reading it.

"Bet you're too chicken to get on a horse aren't you, Hughesy?" Kenny called out. We all started to make clucking noises and pretended to flap our wings.

"Is that Stable Fun Day something to do with you?" asked Emma Hughes, looking down her nose at us.

"Nope!" said Frankie coolly. "We were just reading the poster. We might give it a go though."

"Really?" laughed Emily Berryman in her gruff voice. "Then maybe we should go too, Em, what do you say?" She looked at her friend and they both ran away, giggling.

"What did you say that for?" asked Fliss, going very pink in the face. "We don't want any trouble with them at the Fun Day. They'll spoil everything."

"Not if I have anything to do with it!" shouted Kenny with a nasty gleam in her eye.

But to be honest, we just didn't have time to start worrying about the M&Ms – we had far too much to worry about already!

Adam had got a reply from *The Leicester Mercury* saying that they would be sending a reporter and photographer to cover the Fun Day. And there'd been a couple of mentions of it in the paper already, which was cool. We jumped up and down like monkeys when we read those. But then we started to panic because we'd feel pretty stupid if no one turned up.

As we were trying to show everybody what a great place the riding school was, we had to think of lots of fun things to do. So, as well as gymkhana games, there had to be lots of activities for people who couldn't ride.

We'd agreed that Rosie's mum could take the photographs, then Frankie's parents said they would sell refreshments. That was OK because we thought we'd get bored making tea all day, but when my mum wanted to get involved too it looked as though our parents were going to hijack the day. But Mum is quite laid-back about stuff and said she'd just help where she could, so we agreed that she could have a go at face-painting. Kenny's mum helped us out by persuading local shops to donate prizes for some of the competitions and for a raffle, so that was cool.

I am sure you are wondering what *we* were going to do. Well, Rosie was going to help her mum, Frankie was going to face-paint with mine, and Fliss said that she'd organise the raffle. Kenny thought all those things sounded a bit girlie, so Mrs McAllister said she could help with the gymkhana games. And me? Well, I was actually going to *enter* a couple of the games on Bramble.

I hadn't done anything like that before but fortunately Bramble was an old hand. She's always being entered in gymkhanas so she knew all about stopping and starting and taking corners really tightly. I had to learn everything – including flying dismounts, where you have to leap off while the pony's still moving. Crazy! I wasn't too good at vaulting back on again, though. After a few tumbles, Mrs McAllister suggested that I should enter the sack race and the egg-and-spoon race. Once I'd dismounted in those events, I didn't have to get back on again!

I spent ages riding Bramble across the field so I knew exactly where I would have to turn her and dismount. Then I was like a loony, practising jumping about in a sack and running with an egg balanced on a spoon. And if you've ever done that on sports day, you'll know it's not so easy. Imagine doing it whilst you're leading a pony as well! Mega-crazy!

I had been looking forward to the Fun Day like anything, but when it arrived I was really nervous. I got to the farm early to get Bramble ready. It looked really cool, with flags and garlands everywhere – Mrs McAllister must have put them up the night before. The gymkhana games were being held in one of Mr Brocklehurst's fields and a few stalls had been set up in the practice ring. One of the stables at the riding school, which hadn't been damaged by the fire, was going to be used for refreshments. It had electricity so Mr and Mrs Thomas could boil up lots of water for hot drinks.

When I arrived Bramble was still in the field, so I went to catch her and then took her back to the stable block and gave her a good grooming. It was hard work, but after a while her coat was gleaming! I tacked her up, and then waited for Mrs McAllister to check her over.

"Now remember, Lyndsey, it's not about winning, it's about having fun!" she said, as she tightened Bramble's girth.

I smiled at her, but my stomach was doing somersaults.

"You might as well ride over to the field now," said Mrs McAllister. "Adam and his friends are about to perform in the opening demonstration, then it's your races!"

Once I'd mounted Bramble, I felt a lot calmer. Until, that was, Kenny, Frankie and Rosie came flying towards us.

"Hiya, Lyndz!" they yelled. "Isn't this cool?"

"Are you ready for your races?" asked Frankie.

"I think so," I mumbled.

"Don't worry, you'll thrash them!" Rosie reassured me.

"And I can always help out, if you know what I mean!" laughed Kenny.

"WHOA!" I brought Bramble to a halt. "If I

win I want it to be because I was the best, not because you cheated for me, Kenny!"

"All right, all right!" shouted Kenny. "Don't get your frillies in a flap! I won't help you at all. Promise!"

"Walk on!" I urged Bramble forward again. "Sorry," I told the others. "I'm just a bit nervous!"

As we got close to the field, we saw hundreds of people milling about.

"Wow!" exclaimed Rosie. "Look at those crowds!"

Suddenly there was a blast on a trumpet and a crashing of cymbals and we could see Adam and his friends being led into the field on their horses. Adam and Marvel were at the front. Everybody whooped and cheered and Adam had just the biggest grin on his face.

Looking round at the faces in the crowd, you could tell that everyone was amazed how well someone with cerebral palsy could cope with riding. But, better than that, they could see how much Adam and his friends were enjoying it. Frankie had rushed to grab a tin for collecting donations, and as she worked through the crowd everybody emptied their pockets of change. It was brilliant – and the day had only just started!

"Hey, Lyndz! Over here!" It was Fliss. She was done up like Marge Simpson.

"Oh... hi!" I spluttered. I was almost speechless.

"Isn't it brilliant that so many people have turned up!" she shouted up to me. "Have you seen the photographer from *The Mercury* anywhere? I thought he might want to take a picture of me."

"What, for their Horror Corner?" asked Kenny, who had sneaked up behind her.

"Ha, ha, ha!" snapped Fliss. "I wanted to look my best, that's all!"

Rosie came rushing up. "Does anyone want their photograph taken on Alfie?" she asked. "Mum wants to have a few practice shots before she starts charging anyone!"

"There you go, Fliss, the camera beckons!" I laughed.

"But I don't want to go on a horse!" she yelled.

"Alfie's as gentle as a baby!" I laughed. "Besides, if the photographer from *The Mercury* sees you, he might come and take a few pictures too!"

"Do you think so?" Fliss asked.

"We *know* so," said Kenny, rolling her eyes. "Anyway, Lyndz, I came to tell you that it's time to go into the field. The sack race is starting in two minutes."

I trotted towards the field on Bramble with Kenny running beside me. Fliss and Rosie went to the corner of the other field, where Mrs Cartwright was standing with Alfie and her Polaroid camera.

The sack race was only a fun event and I knew the other three girls who were competing. They were all friendly, so we laughed and pulled faces at each other as Mrs McAllister explained the rules to us.

As I rode over to the starting line, I could hear Kenny and Frankie shouting, "Come on, Lyndz! You can do it!"

I tried to blank everything out of my mind and concentrated on keeping Bramble totally still as we waited behind the line.

When Mrs McAllister lowered her flag, I yelled, "Come on, Bramble! Go, girl!" And we flew to the other end of the field.

I couldn't really see what anyone else was doing, but I knew that we had to do a really tight turn to get back to the centre line. I felt like I was flying. It was wicked! When I could see the centre line approaching, I prepared myself and did the most perfect flying dismount you've ever seen. I was way in front of the others.

"Come on, girl, we've got this won!" I laughed to Bramble.

I was just about to leap into my sack when I heard screaming. I know that I shouldn't have been distracted, but I recognised the scream. It was Fliss. I looked across to the other field and saw that Alfie had broken free and was galloping away. Poor Fliss was slumped across his neck, clinging on for all she was worth.

CHAPTER NINE

OK, so what would you have done? Gone on to win the race, or helped your friend? Yeah right, so a rosette is that important! I dropped my sack, urged Bramble forward and vaulted on to her. And for once I actually made it!

"Come on, girl!" I told her. "This is more important than any sack race!"

There was a gate in the corner of the field. "Kenny, open the gate!" I yelled.

She ran to where I was pointing, undid the catch and pushed the gate open. "Do you know what you're doing?" she shouted to me.

Kenny actually said that! Kenny, the girl who always rushes into things without blinking an eye and thinks about them afterwards!

"I'm not sure," I called back to her. "But I've got to help Fliss!"

I could see Alfie heading towards the bottom end of the field. I couldn't believe that Fliss was still managing to cling on to him. But they were heading for disaster: there were fences on all sides of the field, and I knew that if Alfie was really spooked he might try to jump over one of them. Fliss wouldn't stand a chance then. I urged Bramble towards them as fast as she could go.

"Hang on, Fliss!" I shouted.

Fliss just screamed.

"Try not to scream, Fliss, that'll scare him even more!" I shouted. "Try talking calmly to him."

I could hear Fliss whimpering. Of all the people to be sitting on Alfie when he decided to take off, it had to be Fliss! But I wondered why he'd done it in the first place.

Alfie was usually so calm. Something must have really frightened him to make him bolt like that. *And* he'd been tied up.

"Sit firm in the saddle, Fliss!" I called. "Put all your weight there, and hang on!"

It would have been just my luck for her to fall off as soon as I'd said that. But she didn't, she hung on in there.

I was almost level with them now, and it looked as though Alfie wasn't going to jump over the fence after all. He was slowing down and cantering around the edge of the field. I didn't really know what to do. I didn't want Bramble to get frightened as well; I just wanted to make sure that Alfie was calming down and that Fliss was safe.

I was very relieved when I heard another horse thundering towards us. It was Mrs McAllister on Marvel.

"Whoa, boy!" she said in her quiet, firm voice. She rode alongside Alfie whilst Bramble and I stayed where we were.

When Alfie had slowed down to a walk, she said to Fliss, "Sit tight, I'm going to take his reins."

Fliss stayed where she was. She had been holding on to Alfie's reins as well as his mane, but hadn't known what to do with them. To be honest with you, if the same thing had happened to me, I don't think that I would have been able to stop Alfie either. Mrs McAllister grabbed hold of the loose reins in one hand and gradually circled Alfie round to a stop.

I leapt down from Bramble, and Frankie, Kenny and Rosie came hurtling across the field towards us.

"Are you all right, Fliss!" asked Frankie and Rosie together.

"Wow! That was so cool!" panted Kenny. "You were brill, Fliss, hanging on like that. It was better than a Gladiator challenge! Awesome!"

Mrs McAllister dismounted and asked me to hold Alfie and Marvel, then she went to help Fliss dismount. "That was certainly some riding display!" she said. "I'd say you have a natural talent for this. Have you ever thought of taking it up?"

The rest of us screamed with laughter. I know it sounds awful when Fliss had just gone through such a terrible ordeal and everything, but it was sort of a release after all the excitement. Poor Fliss didn't know whether to laugh or to carry on crying – so she did both!

"Fliss is scared of horses!" I explained.

"In that case you did exceptionally well!" said Mrs McAllister squeezing her shoulder.

We all stopped laughing. The Fun Day would have been a Pretty Miserable Day if Fliss had fallen off and hurt herself. She could have had a terrible accident. It made me go all hot and cold just thinking about it.

"You were really brave, Fliss. Well cool!" I said.

"Yeah, wicked!" said the others.

"Was I?" asked Fliss. She stopped crying and looked up at us. You could tell she was thrilled that we were all praising her. But at the same time, the rest of us knew that she'd be milking this for weeks.

"It just goes to show why you must *always* wear a riding hat when you're on a horse," said Mrs McAllister. "I think I'll have to stop any more children having their photographs taken on the horses and ponies. It's not worth the risk of this happening again."

I was still holding Alfie and Marvel. Mrs McAllister took their reins from me and said, "Round up Bramble, Lyndsey, then we can walk back to the stables. OK, Fliss?"

Fliss nodded and looked all pale and pathetic. The rest of us looked at each other and rolled our eyes, but even we couldn't have a go at her when she'd just had such a terrifying experience.

Bramble was standing quietly, wondering what all the fuss was about. I gathered her reins and followed the others back to the stables. When we got there everybody crowded round us. They wanted to know what had happened and whether Fliss was all right. Even the photographer from *The Mercury* wanted a picture of her, so she was well chuffed about that. He took my photograph too, but I don't know why, just using up film I suppose.

Bramble, Marvel and Alfie loved the attention too. They were patted and stroked and just lapped it all up.

"What I can't understand," said Mrs McAllister thoughtfully, "is how Alfie got in that state in the first place. He's never bolted before. And wasn't he tied up anyway?"

Just then I spotted the M&Ms hanging around, they looked kind of embarrassed.

"I think I've found some people who'll be able to tell you," I said glancing in their direction.

Mrs McAllister took in their guilty-looking faces in a flash and stormed over. "I'd like a word with you, girls," she snapped crossly.

The M&Ms looked terrified as they followed her sheepishly into the stable office.

We tried to sneak up to listen, but I was called for the egg-and-spoon race. To be honest, I didn't feel like competing in another event. But I'd entered and I suppose I still wanted to win a rosette. But Bramble and I were both tired after our rescue mission and we had a disastrous race. I timed my dismount wrong and nearly took a tumble, then I dropped my egg *three* times. Nightmare! It was no surprise when we came in last.

Mrs McAllister had reappeared by the time we'd finished. She was a bit red in the face. The M&Ms were *bright* red and had both been crying. Mrs McAllister ignored them and handed out the rosettes for the sack race and the egg-and-spoon race.

"Never mind, Bramble. Maybe we'll get one next time!" I said as I stroked her muzzle.

"And there's a special rosette here for bravery." Mrs McAllister's voice suddenly caught my attention. "Through the stupidity of various individuals, one of my horses was frightened and ran off with an inexperienced rider on its back. I would just like to stress that this is NOT a common occurrence at my riding school." Everybody laughed. "Lyndsey Collins who was leading the sack race at the time, saw her young friend in difficulties and wasted no time in going to her assistance. She did everything absolutely right, so I would like to award this rosette to Lyndsey Collins and Bramble."

Everybody cheered and clapped like mad. I was embarrassed and thrilled to bits all at the same time, especially when I could hear my crazy friends shouting, "Way to go, Lyndz!"

That was the best bit of the Fun Day for me, but the rest of it was pretty cool too. Everybody seemed to be enjoying themselves, Fliss most of all. People kept stopping her and asking how she was. She just revelled in it and I swear that she developed a limp as the day wore on! The photographer from *The Mercury* took loads more pictures. Fliss tried her best to get in all of them, but the rest of us muscled in on quite a few too!

By the time the Fun Day ended, we were all exhausted. But we hung about as our parents counted up the money. There were huge piles of coins and bundles of notes.

"Wow, we must have raised enough to save the stables now!" squealed Rosie when she saw it all.

Do you know how much we made? Over £400. Our parents kept telling us how brilliant it was, but it wasn't thousands of pounds was it? And that's what Mrs McAllister said she needed to rebuild the stables. All our efforts looked to have been for nothing. No rosette could make up for *that* disappointment.

None of us could have expected what happened next though. And it was certainly a shock to Fliss when she saw her photograph splashed over the front page of *The Mercury* the next day.

CHAPTER TEN

We didn't actually see the paper until the afternoon, but everybody had been talking about the Fun Day at school. It was amazing how many of our class had been there. They all told Fliss how brave she was, which made the rest of us do our 'being sick' impressions, and a few of them told me that I was brave too, which was pretty cool.

The only people who didn't mention the Fun Day were the M&Ms. Mrs McAllister had found out that *they* had untied Alfie whilst Rosie and her mum were getting Fliss ready for having her photograph taken. Then two dogs had begun to fight. And if there's one thing that Alfie's scared of it's dogs. Their snarling must have terrified him and he'd taken off with Fliss on his back.

Mrs McAllister must have bawled the M&Ms out good and proper for the part they'd played in the drama, because they didn't even *look* at us all day.

So we had a pretty cool day at school, and when I got home it got even better. As soon as I got through the door, Mum handed me *The Mercury*. There on the front page was Fliss! But she wasn't looking pretty in all her finery. She was looking like a witch: screaming her head off, with her eyes bulging as she clung on to Alfie. That was one terrific photograph! The caption underneath read: *Brave Felicity Sidebotham clings to a runaway horse during the Fun Day to save McAllister's Riding School.*

"Oh dear," I said to Mum, "that's not exactly good publicity, is it? It sounds as though the whole day was a disaster."

"Turn over," Mum said.

Page two was covered with a whole load of photographs of the Fun Day. There was even one of me with the caption: *Hero of the hour, Lyndsey Collins, who rescued her friend!*

"Coo-el!" I laughed.

On page three there was a report about the Fun Day and why we had organised it. It said: *What a pity it would be if such a vital part of the community was forced to close due to lack of funds.*

At the bottom of the page it said in big letters: *SAVE THE STABLES.* Underneath there was a form to fill in if you wanted to send a donation.

"*The Mercury* is running a campaign for the stables!" I shouted, jumping up and down. "They've got to be saved now haven't they, Mum?"

"I think they probably have, yes!" Mum laughed.

I was still leaping about with excitement when the phone rang.

"Lyndz, Lyndz, have you seen the paper?" It was Frankie. "Isn't it cool? And to think we started it all off!"

No sooner had I got off the phone to Frankie when Kenny rang. "Was that Frankie on the phone? I thought it would be. Isn't it brill? We did it, girl, we saved the stables!"

"We haven't saved them yet!" I laughed. "In fact *we* haven't saved them at all. If anyone's going to save them, it's *The Mercury*."

"Yes, but we *thought* of the Fun Day didn't we? They just took over."

Kenny was right, but the paper could reach a lot more people than we ever could. That's exactly what Rosie had to say when I called her.

"Adam's unbearable!" she laughed. "He keeps telling me that the campaign in *The Mercury* was his idea."

"It doesn't really matter whose idea it was," I said. "As long as it works."

The only person who hadn't rung me was Fliss. So I rang her.

"Isn't it *awful!*" she said when she picked up the phone.

"What?" I asked.

"Isn't my photograph awful!" she said. She sounded really cross. "You'd think they could have used one of the nice ones. They took enough of me!"

"They probably used it for dramatic effect," I told her. "Besides it'll probably boost funds for the campaign. Isn't that a great idea?"

"Yeah, great," Fliss said. "Did I really look that awful, Lyndz?"

What was Fliss like? We had one of our greatest triumphs staring us in the face and all Fliss was bothered about was some crummy photo.

"No, you looked great, Fliss, honestly," I told her.

All week *The Mercury* gave details of how much money people had sent in for the Save the Stables campaign. It seemed a lot, but I still wasn't sure that there was going to be enough. I mean, Mrs McAllister had said that she needed a few thousand pounds to rebuild the stables, and that's an awful lot of money. It would mean everyone who reads *The Mercury* sending in a pound each.

On the Friday after the Fun Day, the rest of the Sleepover Club came round to my house after school. As soon as we piled through the front door we were greeted by my mum. At least we assumed it was my mum. We couldn't see her face because she had a copy of *The Mercury* right in front of it. I know, I know – seriously weird. But the headlines just about stopped us in our tracks: *LOCAL BUSINESSWOMAN SAVES RIDING SCHOOL.*

We all made a grab for the paper.

"Hey, watch it!" laughed Mum. "Let me put it on the table so you can all read it."

Local businesswoman, Sita Chandri, proprietor of Sita's Spices, has agreed to contribute what is needed to rebuild the stable block at McAllister's Riding School. The stables were recently almost destroyed by fire, and The Mercury *has been prominent in running a campaign to prevent their closure due to lack of funds. Mrs Chandri says, 'The spirit of community is very important to me. I felt that I wanted to give something back to the community which has supported me in my business ventures. Paying for the restoration of the stables seemed to be the perfect way to do that.'*

"Way to go, Sita!" shouted Kenny.

We all screamed and hugged each other. It was our idea that had sparked off the whole thing. If we hadn't had our disaster of a sale, we would never have thought about the Fun Day. And if we hadn't had the Fun Day, *The Mercury* would never have got involved and Mrs Chandri might not even have known that the riding school *needed* saving. Wicked!

So that's it, for once we have a happy ending! I'm glad it's all worked out, for Adam's sake as much as mine: he loves the horses almost as much as I do.

*

Sleepover Girls on Horseback

Well, we're finally at the stables. It seems to have taken us ages to get here, doesn't it? Look, Frankie and Rosie are waving at us – what are they like! And Kenny's behaving like a wild animal, as usual. That must be Fliss over there. What is she wearing? Come on, let's find out what they're up to and see if they've any more crazy schemes planned!